The Little Knight Who Battled the Rain

Scholastic Canada Ltd.
Toronto New York London Auckland Sydney
Mexico City New Delhi Hong Kong Buenos Aires

To Mario Desrosiers,
the knight who is afraid of nothing . . .
— GILLES TIBO

To my young knight, Arthur.
— GENEVIÈVE DESPRÉS

Scholastic Canada Ltd.
604 King Street West, Toronto, Ontario M5V 1E1, Canada

Scholastic Inc.
557 Broadway, New York, NY 10012, USA

Scholastic Australia Pty Limited
PO Box 579, Gosford, NSW 2250, Australia

Scholastic New Zealand Limited
Private Bag 94407, Botany, Manukau 2163, New Zealand

Scholastic Children's Books
Euston House, 24 Eversholt Street, London NW1 1DB, UK

www.scholastic.ca

Library and Archives Canada Cataloguing in Publication
Tibo, Gilles, 1951-
[Petit chevalier qui n'aimait pas la pluie. English]
The little knight who battled the rain / Gilles Tibo ; illustrated by
Geneviève Després ; translated by Petra Johannson.
Translation of: Le petit chevalier qui n'aimait pas la pluie.
ISBN 978-1-4431-3382-1 (pbk.)
I. Després, Geneviève, illustrator II. Johannson, Petra, translator
III. Title. IV. Title: Petit chevalier qui n'aimait pas la pluie. English.
PS8589.I26P4313 2015   jC843'.54   C2014-905340-1

6 5 4 3 2 1   Printed in Malaysia 108   15 16 17 18 19

Once upon a time there was a little knight who loved cats, birds and chocolate cake. He wasn't afraid of the dark, or mice, or enemies. The only thing he feared was rain. Rain made his armour rust. Every time a cloud appeared on the horizon, the little knight hid in his fortress and stayed there, trembling, until it was gone.

A stray cat, just passing through.

His helmet is full of holes to let air in.

The dog does not have a name.

The little knight isn't very tall or very big, but he's still the hero of this story.

The little knight's cat, Bartlett.

Three birds singing happily.

His wooden sword is only good for fighting flies.

His pointed shoes help him pick things up without bending down.

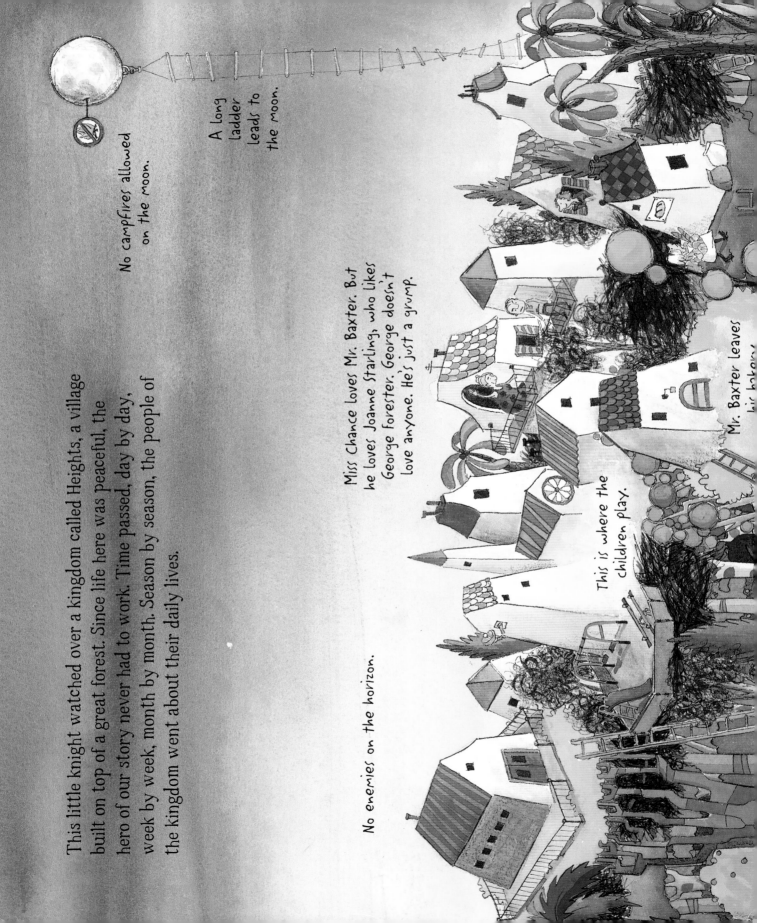

This little knight watched over a kingdom called Heights, a village built on top of a great forest. Since life here was peaceful, the hero of our story never had to work. Time passed, day by day, week by week, month by month. Season by season, the people of the kingdom went about their daily lives.

No campfires allowed on the moon.

A long ladder leads to the moon.

No enemies on the horizon.

Miss Chance loves Mr. Baxter. But he loves Joanne Starling, who likes George Forester. George doesn't love anyone. He's just a grump.

This is where the children play.

Mr. Baxter leaves his bakery.

A small ladder for apple-picking.

The Balko twins and the Singer triplets look for four-leaf clovers.

Two ladders lead to a house.

The ladder leading to the school is very safe.

The little knight munches on a piece of cake as he brushes his horse.

Bartlett tries to catch a frog.

One day, dark clouds appeared on the horizon.
Thunder boomed from the sky. A tremendous
storm descended on the village. Terrified, the
villagers climbed up their long ladders and took
refuge in their homes.

The mice take
shelter under an
umbrella.

The first drop
of rain.

The second drop
of rain.

Bartlett hates
water.

Huge clouds darken the sky.

Lightning zig-zags across the sky.

The thunder goes
BOOM!
BOOM!

Joanne Starling closes her shutters.

The twins hurry up to their hiding place.

Mr. Baxter climbs up to his house.

The third drop of rain.

The triplets scramble away, yelling "Help!"

George Forester runs away, grumbling.

As usual, the little knight fled into the depths of his fortress.
He hid under a pile of pillows, then under his bed, and
finally in a big wardrobe.

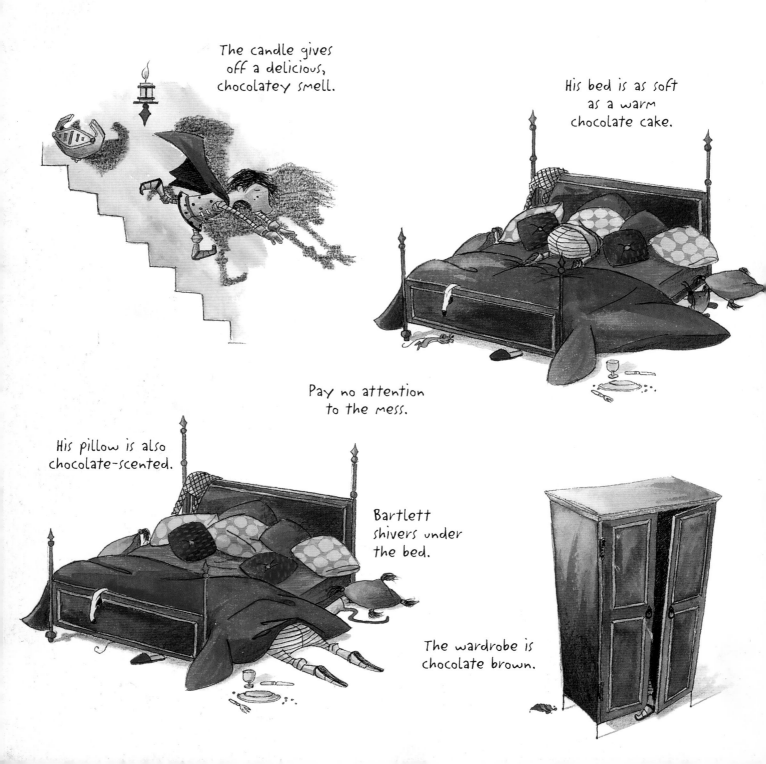

The candle gives
off a delicious,
chocolatey smell.

His bed is as soft
as a warm
chocolate cake.

Pay no attention
to the mess.

His pillow is also
chocolate-scented.

Bartlett
shivers under
the bed.

The wardrobe is
chocolate brown.

There he hid, shaking, eating chocolate cake to forget his fear.

A mouse makes off
with a piece of cake.

The shelves are full of
chocolate cakes.

There was a cherry on
top of this cake, but a
mouse ate it.

Miss Chance's ladder disappears into the distance.

Two millionth drop of rain.

For 39 endless days and nights, rain poured down on the village. For 39 endless days and nights, violent winds whipped the trees. Cracking and groaning, all the kingdom's ladders were torn away. They broke in the fields, shattered against rocks or plunged deep into the sea.

George Forester's ladder flies off into the clouds.

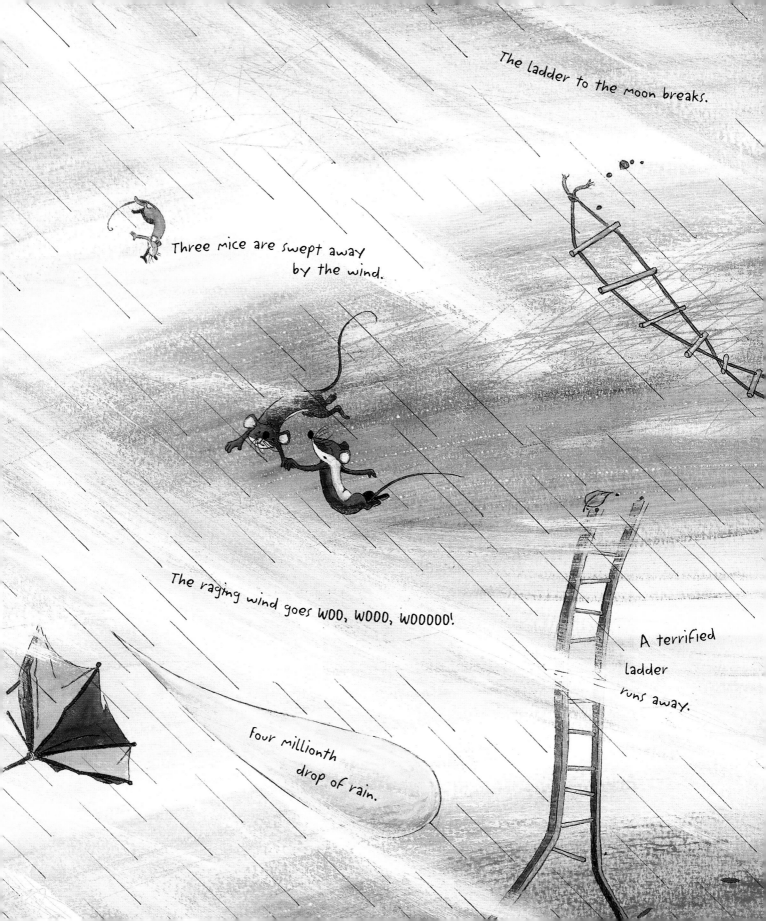

On the morning of the 40th day, the wind stopped blowing.
The storm turned into a light rain. The little knight came
out of his hiding place. He looked outside, wide-eyed. Not a
single ladder remained in the village! People were trapped in
their homes, and everyone was out of food. From balconies,
rooftops and chimneys they cried out:
"HELP! SAVE ME! I'M HUNGRY!"

Bartlett steps outside
the fortress.

The mice return,
without their umbrella.

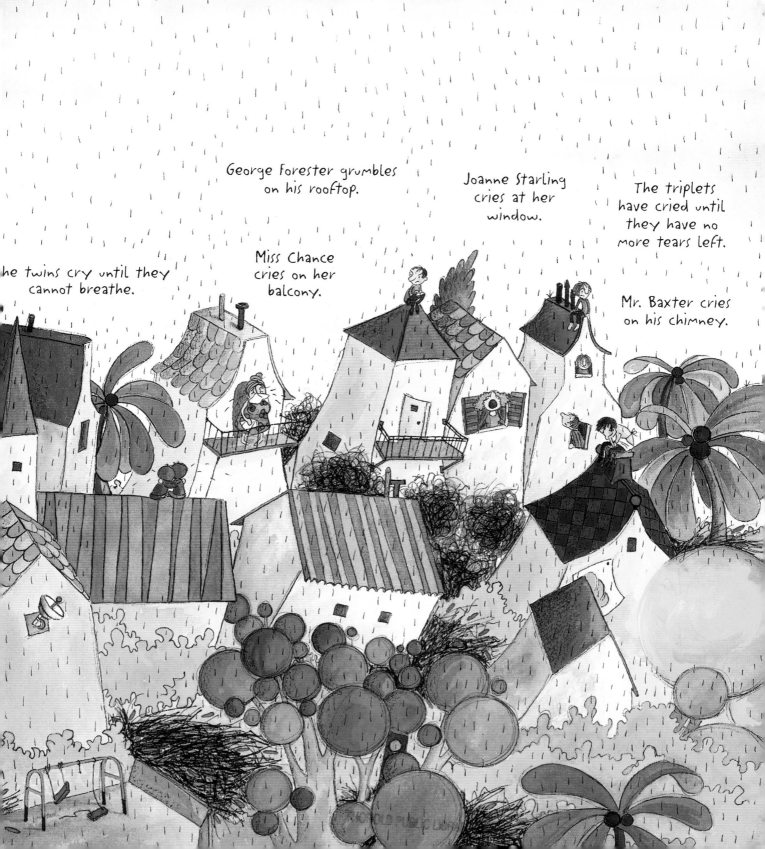

Despite the light rain, the little knight left his fortress, leaped on his horse and rode toward the village. Jumping every time a raindrop fell on his armour, he looked at the damage. Finally, his teeth chattering, he yelled through a bullhorn.

The picnic basket has a new job — now it carries Bartlett.

His horse is not afraid of the water. He knows how to float.

Old-fashioned leather reins have been replaced by handlebars.

A bird lands on the little knight's head.

The mice are hiding somewhere, but where?

The little knight still hates the rain.

"THIS IS YOUR LITTLE KNIGHT! NEVER FEAR!
I WILL FIND A SOLUTION TO HELP YOU ALL!"

The little knight went home, soaked to the skin. He shut himself into his library and read many books of wisdom, but he found nothing. No book had anything on how to save a kingdom that had had its ladders stolen away by the wind. He had to find a solution, and fast, before all the villagers starved to death!

The mice want something to nibble on, but what?

Bartlett dries herself in front of a fan.

The spell books do not have answers for the little knight.

The library is full of books, but they do not answer the little knight's questions.

The wrinkles on the little knight's brow show how troubled he is.

The little knight's sweaty hands show how worried he is.

The little knight abandoned his books and headed to his pantry.
There was nothing left but chocolate, lots and lots of chocolate.
And lots and lots of flour.

Discouraged, he plopped down on a bench. He
tried to find the answer by watching the birds.
He tried to find the answer by looking at the
stove. He tried to find the answer by staring
at his cat. Then, suddenly, as he was thinking
about the cat, the bird and the stove, he cried
out: "I'VE GOT IT!"

The big stove waits
impatiently . . .

Bartlett does not want to
become a chocolate cake.

The birds do not want to become chocolate cake.

The cookbooks are full of good chocolate cake recipes.

The logs wait to be burned.

The mice, who understand nothing, fear nothing.

The little knight climbed onto the roof of his fortress without even hiding under an umbrella. Yelling into his bullhorn, he called all the cats and all the birds of the kingdom. When they came – dozens, hundreds, thousands of them – the little knight asked them to wait. He rushed into the kitchen and threw himself into baking dozens, hundreds, thousands of chocolate cakes.

The little knight mixes flour and chocolate.

The cookbook is stained with chocolate.

The mice nibble on the flour.

The chirping birds wait but do not understand.

Chocolate splatters on the wall.

In his haste, the little knight doesn't worry about the mess.

The mewing cats wait and do not understand.

As the cakes came out of the oven, the little knight gave his orders. The cats and the birds set out from the fortress with big sacks. The cats climbed the trees. The birds flew up to the higher houses. Surprised and happy, the men, women and children of the kingdom stuffed themselves with dozens, hundreds, thousands of chocolate cakes.

Mr. Baxter eats cake happily.

Miss Chance eats cake happily.

The mice nibble cake crumbs happily.

A bird with a heavy sack full of cakes flies up to save the starving villagers.

The twins eat cake happily.

George Forester eats
cake, but he still
grumbles a bit.

A cat with
heavy sack
full of cakes
climbs a tree
to save the
starving
villagers.

Joanne
Starling
eats cake
happily.

The triplets eat
cake happily.

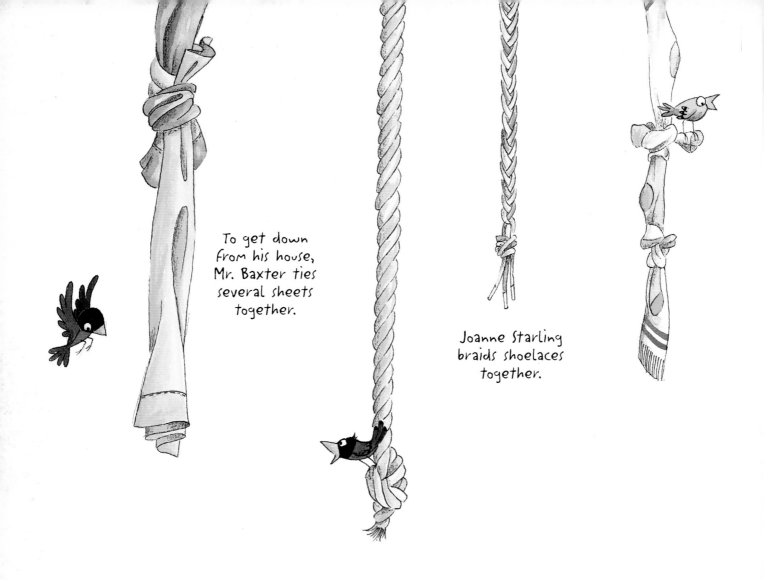

To get down from his house, Mr. Baxter ties several sheets together.

Joanne Starling braids shoelaces together.

Once everyone was full, they began to think about how to get down. They knotted sheets together. They attached socks. They braided shoelaces together. They unravelled sweaters and knit them into ropes.

The first to escape went deep into the forest. They chopped, sawed and nailed. Fuelled by large amounts of cake, they built long ladders, which they attached firmly to the trees and, finally, to the moon.

The twins help build ladders.

The triplets play hopscotch at the base of a huge ladder.

George forester's axe is dull from chopping down so many trees.

This little cloud was not invited to the party.

To thank the little knight, the people organized a party. They ate cake, they laughed and they danced all night. At dawn, lightning flashed across the sky. Thunder boomed over the horizon. A little cloud stopped right above the party and rain began to fall, harder and harder. Everyone took cover in the fortress.

The mice do not know what to do.

The birds fly away.

The cats run away.

The twins flee with their fruit.

The triplets flee with their fruit salad.

Miss Chance, Mr. Baxter, Joanne Starling and George Forester run for their lives.

But oddly, the little knight stayed outside. Alone beneath the cloud, he looked up and smiled. He opened his arms to welcome the first droplets, warm as a summer's day. And the little knight began to laugh and dance . . . he realized that he was no longer afraid of the rain.

Pesky raindrops.

Everyone watches the little knight
from the windows of the fortress.

We can't see
Bartlett. She's
hiding, but
where?

The little knight sings
a little song.

An umbrella
made of
chocolate
cake.

The little knight dances
a little dance.

The little knight was completely happy ... even if
– creak, creak, creak – his armour was starting to rust a bit!